Nick and Nack
Blow
Bubbles

By Brandon Budzi
Art by Charles Lehman

HIGHLIGHTS PRESS

Honesdale, Pennsylvania

Stories + Puzzles = Reading Success!

Dear Parents,

Highlights Puzzle Readers are an innovative approach to learning to read that combines puzzles and stories to build motivated, confident readers.

Developed in collaboration with reading experts, the stories and puzzles are seamlessly integrated so that readers are encouraged to read the story, solve the puzzles, and then read the story again. This helps increase vocabulary and reading fluency and creates a satisfying reading experience for any kind of learner. In addition, solving Hidden Pictures puzzles fosters important reading and learning skills such as:

- letter and shape recognition
- letter-sound relationships
- visual discrimination
- logic
- flexible thinking
- sequencing

With high-interest stories, humorous characters, and trademark puzzles, Highlights Puzzle Readers offer a winning combination for inspiring young learners to love reading.

This is Nick.

This is Nack.

Nick loves to **make** things.
Nack loves to **find** things.
They make a good **team**.

You can help them by solving the **Hidden Pictures** puzzles.

"Here is the soap!" says Nack.

"We will mix the soap with water," says Nick.

"We can put the mix in a pail," says Nack.

Help Nick and Nack.
Find 5 pails hidden in the picture.

Happy reading!

Nick and Nack ride their bicycles.

"Watch out for the puddle!" says Nick.

"Oh no!" says Nack.

SPLOOSH!

"Look at our bicycles!"

says Nack. "They are dirty."

"We can wash them," says Nick.

"Here is soap."

"Here is water," says Nack.

Nick and Nack wash their bicycles.

"Look at the bubbles!" says Nick.

"Can we make more bubbles?"

asks Nack.

"Yes!" says Nick.

"We need to make a wand.

Then we can blow more bubbles."

"What can we use to make a wand?"

asks Nack.

"I need straws," says Nick.

"I will make a big wand.

I want to make big bubbles!"

"I can help find straws," says Nack.

"I found the straws!" says Nack.

"Now I need to make a circle," says Nick.

"Can you use string?" asks Nack.

"Yes!" says Nick.

Help Nick and Nack.
Find 5 balls of string hidden in the picture.

"I will make a little wand," says Nack.

"I want to make little bubbles!"

"Do we have pipe cleaners?"
asks Nick.

"I can help find pipe cleaners,"
says Nack.

"I found pipe cleaners!" says Nack.

"You can bend a pipe cleaner
to make a wand," says Nick.

"Can I also add beads?" asks Nack.

"Yes!" says Nick.

Help Nick and Nack.
Find 5 beads hidden in the picture.

19

"We also need to make bubble mix," says Nack.

"We can use soap," says Nick. "Where did we put the soap?"

"I can help find the soap," says Nack.

Nack finds a scarf.

He finds a sign.

He finds a saw.

He cannot find soap.

"Here is the soap!" says Nack.

"We will mix the soap with water," says Nick.

"We can put the mix in a pail," says Nack.

Help Nick and Nack.
Find 5 pails hidden in the picture.

Soap

"First, we can make the wands!"
says Nick.

He makes a big wand.

Nack makes a little wand.

"Our wands are done!" says Nick.

"Now we can make the bubble mix."

Nick fills up the pail with water.

Then Nick adds the soap.

They stir the bubble mix.

"Time to blow bubbles!" says Nick.

"Look!" says Nack.

"I blew a little bubble."

"Look!" says Nick.

"I blew a big bubble."

"How can we blow

more bubbles?" asks Nack.

"We can use a fan!" says Nick.

Help Nick and Nack.
Find 5 fans hidden in the picture.

Blow Your Own
BUBBLES!

Nick's Bubble Wand

WHAT YOU NEED:

- 2 straws
- String
- Scissors

1 Cut a piece of string six times as long as the length of a straw.

2 Thread the string through the two straws.

3 Tie the ends of the string together. Slide the knot into one of the straws.

4 Hold the straws as handles. Dip the wand and your hands into the bubble mix to create large bubbles.

BUBBLE MIX

WHAT YOU NEED:

- Pail
- 3 cups of "soft" or distilled water
- 6 tablespoons of dish detergent
- 3 tablespoons of glycerin or corn syrup

1. Put the "soft" or distilled water in a clean bucket.

2. Add the dish detergent and glycerin or corn syrup.

3. Gently stir the mixture. Try not to create suds.

4. Let the mixture sit for a few hours or overnight before using.

Nack's Bubble Wand

WHAT YOU NEED:

Pipe cleaner

Beads

This wand is a circle, but you can make any shape you want, like a heart or a triangle.

1 Create a loop at the top of a chenille stick. Twist the end of the loop around the handle to hold the loop in place.

2 Add beads onto the end of the chenille stick.

3 Tuck the end of the pipe cleaner into the bottom bead. Have fun blowing small bubbles!

Nick and Nack's TIPS

- Gather your supplies before you start crafting.
- Ask an adult or robot for help with anything sharp or hot.
- Clean up your workspace when your craft is done.

For information about permission to reprint
selections from this book, please contact
permissions@highlights.com.

Published by Highlights Press
815 Church Street
Honesdale, Pennsylvania 18431
ISBN (paperback): 978-1-64472-194-0
ISBN (hardcover): 978-1-64472-195-7
ISBN (ebook): 978-1-64472-239-8

Library of Congress Control Number: 2020949551
Printed in Melrose Park, IL, USA
Mfg. 03/2021
First edition
Visit our website at Highlights.com.
10 9 8 7 6 5 4 3 2 1

Craft instructions by Elizabeth Wyrsch-Ba
Craft samples by Lisa Glover
Photos by Jim Filipski, Guy Cali Associates, Inc.

This book has been officially leveled by using the
F&P Text Level Gradient™ Leveling System.

LEXILE®, LEXILE FRAMEWORK® ,
LEXILE ANALYZER®, the LEXILE®
logo and POWERV® are trademarks of
MetaMetrics, Inc., and are registered
in the United States and abroad. The
trademarks and names of other companies and
products mentioned herein are the property of their
respective owners. Copyright © 2021 MetaMetrics,
Inc. All rights reserved.

For assistance in the preparation of this book,
the editors would like to thank Vanessa Maldonado,
MSEd, MS Literacy Ed. K–12, Reading/LA Consultant
Cert., K–5 Literacy Instructional Coach; and
Gina Shaw.